THE ADVENTURES OF

ALI BABA
BERNSTEIN

Other Scholastic Books by Johanna Hurwitz

Aldo Applesauce
DeDe Takes Charge!
The Hot and Cold Summer
Tough-Luck Karen
What Goes Up Must Come Down

THE ADVENTURES OF

ALI BABA BERNSTEIN

BY
JOHANNA HURWITZ

ILLUSTRATED BY GAIL OWENS

SCHOLASTIC INC.
New York Toronto London Auckland Sydney

No part of this publication may be reproduced in whole or in part,
or stored in a retrieval system, or transmitted in any form or
by any means, electronic, mechanical, photocopying, recording,
or otherwise, without written permission of the publisher.
For information regarding permission, write to
William Morrow & Company, 105 Madison Avenue, New York, NY 10016.

ISBN 0-590-42011-9

Copyright © 1985 by Johanna Hurwitz.
All rights reserved. Published by Scholastic Inc.,
730 Broadway, New York, NY 10003, by arrangement with
William Morrow & Company. LUCKY STAR is a trademark of Scholastic Inc.

12 11 10 9 8 7 6 5 4 3   9/8 0 1 2 3/9

Printed in the U.S.A.   11

First Scholastic printing, February 1987

To the Rogovins,
for all our shared memories

CONTENTS

1. HOW ALI BABA GOT HIS NAME

David Bernstein was eight years, five months, and seventeen days old when he chose his new name.

There were already four Davids in David Bernstein's third-grade class. Every time his teacher, Mrs. Booxbaum, called, "David," all four boys answered. David didn't like that one bit. He wished he had an exciting name like one of the explorers he learned about in social studies—Vasco Da Gama. Once he found two unusual names on a program his parents brought home from a concert—Zubin Mehta and Wolfgang Amadeus Mozart. Now those were names with pizzazz!

David Bernstein might have gone along forever being just another David if it had not been for the book report that his teacher assigned.

"I will give extra credit for fat books," Mrs. Booxbaum told the class.

She didn't realize that all of her students would try to outdo one another. That afternoon when the third grade went to the school library, everyone tried to find the fattest book.

Melanie found a book with eighty pages.

Sam found a book with ninety-seven pages.

Jeffrey found a book with one hundred nineteen pages.

David K. and David S. each took a copy of the same book. It had one hundred forty-five pages.

None of the books were long enough for David Bernstein. He looked at a few that had over one hundred pages. He found one that had two hundred fourteen pages. But he wanted a book that had more pages than the total of all the pages in all the books his classmates were reading. He wanted to be the best student in the class—even in the entire school.

That afternoon he asked his mother what the fattest book was. Mrs. Bernstein thought for a minute. "I guess that would have to be the Manhattan telephone book," she said.

David Bernstein rushed to get the phone book. He lifted it up and opened to the last page. When he saw that it had over 1,578 pages, he was delighted.

He knew that no student in the history of P.S. 35 had ever read such a fat book. Just think how much extra credit he would get! David took the book and began to read name after name after name. After turning through all the *A* pages, he skipped to the name Bernstein. He found the listing for his father, Robert Bernstein. There were fifteen of them. Then he counted the number of David Bernsteins in the telephone book. There were seventeen. There was also a woman named Davida and a man named Davis, but he didn't

count them. Right at that moment, David Bernstein decided two things: he would change his name and he would find another book to read.

The next day David went back to the school library. He asked the librarian to help him pick out a very fat book. "But it must be very exciting, too," he told her.

"I know just the thing for you," said the librarian.

She handed David a thick book with a bright red cover. It was *The Arabian Nights*. It had only three hundred thirty-seven pages, but it looked a lot more interesting than the phone book. David checked the book out of the library and spent the entire evening reading it. When he showed the book to his teacher the next day, she was very pleased.

"That is a good book," she said. "David, you have made a fine choice."

It was at that moment that David Bernstein announced his new name. He had found it in the library book.

"From now on," David said, "I want to be called Ali Baba Bernstein."

Mrs. Booxbaum was surprised. David's parents were even more surprised. "David is a beautiful name," said his mother. "It was my grandfather's name."

"You can't just go around changing your name when you feel like it," his father said. "How will I ever know who I'm talking to?"

"You'll know it's still me," Ali Baba told his parents.

Mr. and Mrs. Bernstein finally agreed, although both of them frequently forgot and called their son David.

So now in Mrs. Booxbaum's class, there were three Davids and one Ali Baba. Ali Baba Bernstein was very happy. He was sure that a boy with an exciting name would have truly exciting adventures.

Only time would tell.

2. ALI BABA AND THE SECRET TREASURE

The first Ali Baba—the one Ali Baba Bernstein had read about in his library book—found a robber's treasure. He knew the magic words to open a secret cave and he knew how to trick the wicked robbers. Nothing like that ever happened to Ali Baba Bernstein. Five days a week he went to school. Third grade was not very different from second grade, even if the work was a little harder. The kids were the same and the games they played at recess or in phys ed were about the same, too.

Sometimes on the weekends Ali Baba rode the subway to his grandparents' house. As the train rumbled along and the lights in the dark tunnel flickered on and off, Ali Baba would pretend the train had crossed onto a secret track. Maybe they were all heading to a mysterious cave deep underground where robbers had hidden gold and jewels. The speeding train would begin to slow down as it approached a station. Ali Baba hoped it would be a station where no train had ever stopped before. But then he looked out the train window. The sign read: SIXTY-SIXTH STREET, where his grandparents lived.

"I thought having a name like Ali Baba would make things pick up around here," Ali Baba complained to his mother. "But I still keep doing David sort of things."

"Changing your name won't make your life any different," Mrs. Bernstein said. "It won't make you grow up any faster. This year you can cross Broadway by yourself," his mother reminded him. "You can walk to Roger

Zucker's house all alone. Last year you thought that was a big deal."

It was true. A year ago, crossing Broadway, a two-way street with lots of traffic, *had* seemed like a big adventure. Now that he could actually do it, Ali Baba longed for bigger adventures than just crossing the street.

One Saturday morning when Ali Baba Bernstein was eight years, six months, and twenty-three days old, his mother asked him to help her carry the laundry down to the basement of their apartment building, where there were washing machines and dryers. Mrs. Bernstein began to load two of the machines with laundry, but she realized that she'd forgotten the detergent.

"David, will you watch our laundry while I go get the soap?"

"My name is Ali Baba," he corrected her. "Don't worry about the laundry." Who in the world would want to steal their dirty clothes?

Mrs. Bernstein went to the elevator and Ali Baba sat down near the washing machines. But after a moment or two he got up and started to look around. The dim, slightly damp basement was a little like a cave, he thought.

In one corner of the basement was the furnace that heated the building during the winter and made the hot water. Ali Baba could hear the furnace's motor and the whole area around it was hot. It didn't exactly frighten him, but he decided he would rather explore another part of the basement instead. This was where people in the building stored their old furniture, bikes, baby carriages, suitcases, and anything else that they didn't need but didn't want to get rid of. The storage area was divided into cages with heavy mesh wiring between each cage. Ali Baba had been inside the cage where the Bernsteins kept their castoffs. He peeked in now and tried the door to the cage but it was locked. Through the wire mesh, he could see his old tricycle from when he was little and even his crib, which stood in pieces leaning against someone else's table.

Ali Baba walked down the row of cages, trying each door as he went past. He didn't expect any of the doors to be open, but he tried anyway. At the very end of the row, he found one door that was unlocked. He went inside.

There were old chairs covered with dusty velvet and three big, old-fashioned trunks, like the ones Ali Baba had seen in movies. He didn't know anyone who owned anything like them. It didn't seem like snooping to open them, especially when the lids on the trunks lifted so easily. Ali Baba wrinkled his nose at the odor of mothballs. The first two trunks contained old clothing. He almost didn't open the third trunk. But he knew the first Ali Baba would never leave a trunk unexplored so he decided to take a peek. Even in the dim light, he had no trouble seeing what was in the third trunk. It was filled with sparkling diamonds, rubies, pearls, and gold chains.

Ali Baba could hardly believe his eyes. He closed the lid and read the label with the owner's name: VIVALDI. Who was that?

"David, David," a voice called. It was his mother returning to the basement with the soap. Ali Baba was so stunned by what he had found in the third trunk that he didn't even correct her when she used his old name. All he could think about was the jewels. He was about to tell his mother everything but he stopped just in time. She might say that he had no business poking into other people's trunks.

At lunchtime, Ali Baba was still wondering about the jewels. Why would anyone keep a treasure in the basement? It must be that the owner of the jewels did not want anyone to find them inside his apartment. The more he thought about it, the more certain he was that he had stumbled on a stolen treasure. He wished he could talk about this with his friend Roger Zucker. Maybe the two of them could solve the mystery together. Unfortunately Roger and his family had gone away for the weekend. Ali Baba would have to get to the bottom of this mystery by himself. He would make sure the jewels were returned to their rightful owners. He would be a hero just like the first Ali Baba!

After lunch, Ali Baba's mother asked him to go get the mail. Although there was rarely any mail for him, this was a chore Ali Baba enjoyed. Today he studied all the names on all the other mail boxes in the lobby. Box 4K was labeled VIVALDI. There was no question about it. The thief lived right in this building!

"Did you ever hear the name Vivaldi?" Ali Baba asked his parents when he returned with the mail.

"Of course," said his mother. "He's an Italian composer of baroque music."

"Does he have a police record?" asked Ali Baba.

"Not that I know of. He's been dead at least two hundred years."

"I don't think we're talking about the same man," said Ali Baba. The jewels in the basement couldn't have been there that long. The building was only fifty years old.

"There's someone named Vivaldi living in this building," said Mr. Bernstein, looking up from the letter he was reading. "I met him at a tenants' meeting. He was worried that he wouldn't be able to buy his apartment if our building was turned into a co-op. I told him that as a senior citizen he couldn't be evicted."

A thief should be evicted, Ali Baba thought darkly. But he didn't say anything.

That afternoon Mrs. Bernstein sent Ali Baba to the store on the corner. She needed eggs for a recipe she wanted to try. Ali Baba was glad to go. On the way back he could check up on Mr. Vivaldi. Ali Baba rode the elevator down to the street and rushed to get the eggs. When he returned to the building, he got off the elevator at the fourth floor.

Even as he was coming out of the elevator, Ali Baba could hear a woman screaming. As he approached the door of 4K, he heard the woman's screams come from inside the apartment. Ali Baba stood frozen. Did Mr. Vivaldi lure women with jewels into his apartment and rob them? The woman screamed again.

Why couldn't any of Mr. Vivaldi's neighbors hear her? The woman shrieked louder. Without thinking, Ali Baba banged on Mr. Vivaldi's door. He didn't have any weapon on him. All he had was a dozen eggs. If he had to, he could throw them at Mr. Vivaldi.

"Open the door!" shouted Ali Baba.

Slowly the apartment door opened. Ali Baba was about to rush inside, but one look at the man in the doorway stopped him.

He had on a helmet, but it didn't look like the kind football players wore. He was holding a shield, and there was a sword hanging from his waist.

The woman shrieked again. Ali Baba remembered why he was there. "I'll save you," Ali Baba cried and pushed his way into the apartment. He could hear the woman, but he couldn't see her.

"Where did you hide her?" Ali Baba demanded. He pulled the carton of eggs out of the paper bag. If Mr. Vivaldi drew his sword, he would throw it in his face.

"Is she in the bathroom?"

"What's wrong with you, young man?" asked Mr. Vivaldi.

"What's wrong with *me*?" Ali Baba said. "You're the one who steals women's jewels. Shame on you. You should be in jail."

Mr. Vivaldi walked over to his phonograph and turned it off. Suddenly the room was

quiet. There was no more shrieking.

"Who are you?" asked the man. "Will you please tell me what this is all about?"

Ali Baba held the carton of eggs ready, just in case. "I heard a woman screaming in here," he said. "I want to know where she is."

"I think you mean *Norma,*" said the man.

"Aha!" said Ali Baba. "I knew it. Don't try any of your tricks."

"*Norma* is the name of an opera. The role was sung by Maria Callas."

"Maria?" echoed Ali Baba. "How many women do you have stashed in this apartment?"

"Alas," sighed Mr. Vivaldi. "Maria Callas is dead. It is a great loss to the world."

"You should have thought of that before you killed her," Ali Baba said. "Don't make a move, or I'll throw these eggs at you. I'm going to call the police."

Ali Baba edged toward the telephone. He remembered that the number for emergencies was 911.

"I didn't kill her," said Mr. Vivaldi. "That was a role I never got."

17

"Then who did?" demanded Ali Baba. "Do you have an accomplice? And where did you get all those jewels I saw in the basement?"

Mr. Vivaldi sat down on his sofa. "I'm sorry. I think there has been a misunderstanding," he said.

"It's too late for excuses, Mr. Vivaldi."

"Please," the man said. "Put down those eggs before you drop them on my carpet. I'll tell you everything."

Reluctantly Ali Baba put down the eggs. If Mr. Vivaldi lunged forward with his sword, Ali Baba would have to move very quickly.

"For many years I sang with the opera," said Mr. Vivaldi. "I had many fine roles. Now I am too old to sing onstage. But I still listen to my operas on the phonograph. I like to pretend that I'm singing before an audience. That's why I've kept my old costumes."

"I didn't think you bought that outfit at a department store," said Ali Baba.

Mr. Vivaldi smiled. "You heard me playing the opera *Norma*. To you, I guess, it did sound like someone screaming. But what you actually heard was the voice of Maria Callas."

"The one who's dead?" asked Ali Baba.

Mr. Vivaldi nodded.

"Then there aren't any women in the apartment with you?" Ali Baba didn't know if he was relieved or disappointed.

"That is correct, young man."

"But what about the jewels?" asked Ali Baba. "I saw them with my own eyes in the trunk in the basement. Who did you steal them from?"

"I think you are referring to the fake jewelry we used on the stage," said Mr. Vivaldi. "Alas, none of it is worth a penny."

"You mean those aren't real diamonds and rubies?"

Mr. Vivaldi shook his head.

"Gee," said Ali Baba. "I never saw so many jewels before. I was sure you were a robber." He looked the old man straight in the eye. "Are you sure you aren't lying to me?"

"Young man," said Mr. Vivaldi, "you flatter me. Imagine thinking I was young enough to be a jewel thief. You make me feel seventy again! And I'm going to be eighty-three on my next birthday."

"Gee," said Ali Baba. "That's really old."

"So it is," said Mr. Vivaldi. "How old are you?"

"Eight years, six months, and twenty-three days," said Ali Baba.

"That's a good age," said Mr. Vivaldi. "What is your name? You never told me."

"Ali Baba. Ali Baba Bernstein."

"Interesting name. Well, Ali Baba, now that we are properly introduced, come another day if you would like. We can listen to *Carmen* together."

Ali Baba got ready to leave. He knew his mother would be wondering where he was.

As he waited for the elevator, Ali Baba could hear the phonograph playing again in apartment 4K. This time a man was singing. Ali Baba wondered if that was the way Mr. Vivaldi used to sound. He stood listening to the music until the elevator came.

3. ALI BABA AND THE FORTY SLEEVES

One Saturday when Ali Baba Bernstein was eight years, seven months, and four days old, he went to play at his friend Roger's house. Ali Baba's parents were going out that evening and it had been arranged that he would spend the night at the Zuckers'. It was a plan that suited Ali Baba just fine. He felt he was too old for baby-sitters.

"Hi, David," Roger greeted his friend at the door.

"Ali Baba. How many times do I have to tell you?"

"Sorry," said Roger, grinning. Ali Baba had tried and tried to get Roger to change his name to Sinbad. "Then we can both have exciting adventures." But Roger held firm. He had always been Roger, and Roger he would remain. He liked his name.

"My parents are having a party tonight," Roger told Ali Baba.

"Who's coming?" asked Ali Baba. "Anybody interesting?"

"Naw," said Roger. "But there's going to be a lot of good food from my father's store."

Roger's father owned a store called Cheese Heaven. Ali Baba hoped heaven didn't smell like Roger's father's store. The store also sold fancy chocolates, and Ali Baba had no complaints about them.

"Woody Allen once bought cheese from my father," Roger said. Now Roger went to see every Woody Allen movie that came out, and he liked to brag to his friend about the gorgonzola that the actor had purchased at Cheese Heaven.

"Is he coming to the party?" asked Ali Baba hopefully.

"Naw," said Roger. "He's probably giving a party himself with the cheese he bought." Since it was over a year since Woody Allen had made his purchase at Cheese Heaven, Ali Baba had his doubts about that. But he didn't say so to Roger.

The two boys spent the afternoon playing FBI. Even though Mr. Vivaldi had proven himself innocent, Ali Baba felt sure there were many criminals still lurking about. First the boys rode up and down in the elevator of Roger's apartment building looking for anything suspicious. Then they checked the halls. Mrs. Zucker was busy getting ready for her guests, and she didn't mind the boys playing in the hallway.

There were two newspapers in front of apartment 7G. "I bet those people skipped town," said Ali Baba.

"Maybe they just don't want to read the news," said Roger.

In front of apartment 9B, there was a broken bottle of ketchup and two broken eggs.

"Looks like someone dropped their groceries," said Roger.

Ali Baba bent over and examined the mess on the floor.

"It may be blood," he said. "They could have broken the ketchup bottle to cover it up."

"What about the eggs?" asked Roger.

"It's all supposed to throw us off the track."

"What track?" asked Roger.

"The track of the murderer," said Ali Baba. But just then the door of apartment 9B opened and a woman stepped out holding some paper towels.

"Would you boys please give me a hand?" she asked. "I dropped my groceries and it made a mess here."

The boys found themselves wiping up the ketchup and eggs.

"Be careful not to cut yourself on the glass," the woman warned them—as if FBI agents needed to be told a thing like that.

"Let's get out of here," said Ali Baba when they finished cleaning the floor. "Maybe something suspicious is happening on the thirteenth floor."

The building where Ali Baba lived didn't even have a thirteenth floor. A lot of buildings didn't because people were superstitious. The floor numbers went up to twelve and then skipped to fourteen. Unfortunately there was no blood and not even any ketchup on the thirteenth floor of Roger's building today. In disgust the boys returned to Roger's apartment. Maybe there was something good to watch on TV.

Mrs. Zucker was putting Roger's baby sister Sugar to bed. Sugar was thirteen months old and her real name was Sarah. The boys had to have supper early because of the party. "You two can play in Roger's room after dinner," Mrs. Zucker told them. "I'll bring you some party food later."

Ali Baba was disappointed that he wasn't invited to the party. You could never tell who might turn up among the guests.

Mr. Zucker was in the kitchen unwrapping packages of cheese that he had brought home from his store.

"I always get a little nervous when the Whitestones are coming," Mrs. Zucker said to her husband. "That Eddie is such a joker. He always seems to have something up his sleeve."

"What do you mean?" asked Ali Baba. He wondered what kind of things Eddie Whitestone might have up his sleeve.

"Oh, it's just an expression," laughed Mrs. Zucker. "Finish up, boys. I want to clear away these dishes."

Reluctantly Ali Baba finished his glass of milk. He wanted to know more about Eddie Whitestone.

The boys were just sitting down to a game of Monopoly when Mrs. Zucker came to the door of Roger's room. "Would you boys like to help out at the party?" she asked. "You can take the guests' coats and put everything on my bed."

"Oh, Mom," Roger started to complain, but Ali Baba nudged him and quickly said,

"Sure, Mrs. Zucker. We'd be glad to." Now he would get a good look at Eddie Whitestone and the other guests, too.

The Zuckers' guests began arriving around eight o'clock. Ali Baba and Roger stood near the door and took the heavy winter coats from people as they entered. Ali Baba looked at everyone closely. He wondered if he'd be able to spot Eddie Whitestone and whatever he had up his sleeve.

"Be sure and point out this Whitestone fellow," he told Roger.

"I don't see why you're so interested in him," sighed Roger.

More and more guests kept arriving. The Zuckers were expecting twenty people. A beautiful woman with long blond hair arrived. She looked like a movie actress. She smelled like flowers. Ali Baba was sure she must be someone very special. Maybe she really was a movie actress. "Who's that?" he whispered into Roger's ear.

"That's LuLu," Roger whispered back.

Ali Baba nodded his head. The name matched its owner perfectly.

LuLu was wearing a fur coat that almost touched the floor. She shook her hair back off her face as she handed her coat to Ali Baba.

"My, aren't you a handsome young man," she said smiling at him.

Ali Baba was so busy looking at LuLu and smelling her perfume that he hardly noticed the man standing next to her. Roger took his coat and muffler and the two of them walked into the living room together. "Well," said Roger, "now you saw Eddie Whitestone."

Ali Baba stared hard at the man who was entering the living room. His head had been shaved so there wasn't a single hair on it, but he had a bushy moustache. There was something very suspicious about him. Ali Baba was sure of that.

Before long the queen-size bed in Roger's parents' bedroom was piled high with the coats of all the guests.

Mr. Zucker came into the bedroom to thank them. "You fellows can go back to your game now," he said. "Everyone's here."

The boys returned to Roger's room, and

Roger began counting the Monopoly money into piles. "Do you want to be the banker?" Roger asked.

Ali Baba shook his head. He didn't want to play Monopoly at all. He wanted to watch the people at the party. He just knew that Eddie Whitestone had something up his sleeve and he wanted to find out what it was. "Could we go to the kitchen for a drink of water?" he suggested to Roger.

"There's water in the bathroom," said Roger, still counting out the play money.

"Aren't you curious about what they're doing out there?" asked Ali Baba.

"I know what they're doing," said Roger. "I've peeked out at other parties. All they ever do at parties is talk, talk, talk. They tell jokes that aren't funny. They drink and smoke and eat. A grown-up party isn't nearly as much fun as a kid's party."

There was a knock on Roger's door. He opened it and Mrs. Zucker was standing there.

"Did you bring us something to eat?" asked Roger.

"Not yet," said his mother. "But I have a favor to ask of you boys. LuLu has lost one of her diamond earrings. She thinks it might have happened while she was taking off her coat. Would you please look for it?"

"Sure!" said Ali Baba jumping up. This had to be better than Monopoly.

"I bet Eddie Whitestone stole it," he said to himself. He wondered how you could steal an earring out of a woman's ear? Maybe Eddie had pretended to kiss her and secretly removed it.

"LuLu took off her coat at the door," Roger remembered. "We should start there."

In front of the door, the boys got down on their hands and knees and began to feel around, but there was nothing but carpet on the floor.

"It might be in the bedroom with the coats," Ali Baba told Roger. "I have a hunch we'll find the earring there." He didn't say it, but he was sure it would be in Eddie Whitestone's sleeve.

Roger followed Ali Baba into the bedroom.

He got down on the floor and began feeling around under the bed.

Ali Baba lifted the top coat from the bed. He didn't know what coat Eddie Whitestone had been wearing. He would have to look through them all. He put his hand into one coat sleeve. There was nothing in it. "I'll dump the coats on the floor until I'm finished," he told Roger who was still down there crawling around.

"Maybe we'll get a reward if we find it," said Roger. "How much do you think a diamond earring is worth?"

"A million dollars," Ali Baba guessed as he lifted the next coat. It was a woman's fur coat. Eddie Whitestone probably wouldn't have hidden the diamond in someone else's coat, but you could never tell. The FBI would certainly leave no sleeve untouched if they were called in on this case. Ali Baba reached into one and then the other sleeve of the fur coat and pulled out a silk scarf that smelled wonderfully of perfume. It was LuLu's coat. He recognized the smell.

Roger got up from the floor and began helping. He shook out a navy blue coat. "Look inside the sleeves," Ali Baba told him.

"How would an earring get inside a sleeve?" asked Roger.

"If someone put it there, it would get inside," said Ali Baba.

"You're crazy," said Roger.

Ali Baba did not give up. He stuck his hands into sleeve after sleeve. He was convinced that the diamond earring was in the room with them. And he was determined to find it and to expose Eddie Whitestone as the thief.

He came to a dark gray coat with a fur collar. Following the same routine he had used with the other coats, he shook it out carefully. Then he put his hands into the sleeves. There was a soft wool muffler in the right sleeve. He pulled it out to examine it. And there, just as he had known it would be, was the sparkling diamond earring stuck in the wool.

"I found it!" he shouted. "Look. Here it is!" he climbed over the coats on the floor to show Roger.

"Fantastic!" said Roger. "Let's go show everyone."

"No, wait. I think you'd better call your parents in here first."

Roger looked puzzled, but he left the room and returned with both of his parents.

"I wanted you to see this," said Ali Baba holding out the muffler. He had put the earring in his pocket for safekeeping.

"Why, that's Eddie Whitestone's muffler," said Mr. Zucker.

"Exactly," said Ali Baba. "You said Eddie Whitestone always had something up his sleeve, and that's just where I found this muffler. And look what was stuck into it!" Ali Baba whipped out the diamond.

"Oh, David," Mrs. Zucker exclaimed. "You found it! LuLu will be thrilled. Eddie just gave her those earrings for their anniversary."

Ali Baba turned deep red. It had never occurred to him that LuLu could be married to Eddie Whitestone.

"How clever of you to find the earring," said Mrs. Zucker, putting her arm around Ali

Baba. "Let's stick it back on the muffler, as it was. Everyone will be so surprised."

Ali Baba followed the Zuckers out of the bedroom. The guests were sitting around talking, but they all turned when the four of them walked into the living room.

"Look what we found," shouted Roger.

"Why that's my muffler," said Eddie White-stone, pulling on his moustache.

"Oh, look," cried LuLu. "My diamond earring. It must have gotten caught on Eddie's muffler when we were taking off our coats."

She picked the earing out of the woolen scarf and stuck it back into her earlobe.

"Roger, you're wonderful," she said, giving him a big kiss on his cheek.

Roger blushed. "It wasn't me," he said. "It was Ali Baba!"

Before he knew what was happening, Ali Baba found himself wrapped in LuLu's arms. She kissed him on both cheeks and left lipstick smudges.

Then with her arm still around Ali Baba, Lu Lu turned to her husband. "Eddie," she said.

"I think these boys should get a reward for their detective work."

Eddie Whitestone walked over to them. He took his wallet out of his pants pocket and removed two bills.

"This is for the two of you," he said. He handed each boy a five-dollar bill. "And many thanks for finding the earring."

The guests all burst into applause.

Mrs. Zucker handed Roger a plate on which she had piled an assortment of goodies. The boys took the food and the money and returned to Roger's room. It was almost time for bed.

Ali Baba was glad to have missed their game of Monopoly. Real money was better than Monopoly money any day of the week.

4. ALI BABA AND PRINCESS FARRAH

One Sunday when Ali Baba was eight years, nine months, and nineteen days old, his parents took him to visit the Fishbones. The Fishbones were friends of his parents and had a daughter named Valerie. Ali Baba had never met Valerie, but she was his age. At least that was what Mrs. Bernstein had told Ali Baba when they set out for the visit. They hadn't been at the Fishbones five minutes before Ali Baba learned Valerie's true age. She was seven years, two months, and no days. He had been tricked. The Fishbones had an unusual name, but they seemed quite ordinary. Ali Baba hoped his parents would be ready to go home soon. He didn't want to waste an entire Sunday afternoon.

"I know you are going to enjoy playing with Valerie," Mrs. Fishbone told Ali Baba. "She's very good at games. She even beat me at Scrabble last week." Mrs. Fishbone turned to Ali Baba's mother and said proudly, "Did I tell you that Valerie's reading scores are in the ninety-ninth percentile?"

Ali Baba didn't know what that meant, but it didn't make him feel any better about Valerie.

"Valerie, why don't you show David your games," Mrs. Fishbone suggested.

"Ali Baba," he corrected her.

Mrs. Fishbone looked puzzled.

"Our son has chosen a new name this year," Mrs. Bernstein explained. "He didn't want to be just another David."

Reluctantly Ali Baba followed Valerie to her bedroom. She had the usual games: Monopoly, Clue, Chinese checkers. Nothing very exciting. She also had a whole shelf lined with dolls. Ugh. What a wasted afternoon, he thought. Then he noticed a small glass tank on the chest of drawers. Inside there was some dirt and a couple of small rocks. A tiny green frog perched on one of the rocks.

"Can I pick him up?" Ali Baba asked.

"It's not a boy, it's a girl. Her name is Farrah." Valerie removed the netting that covered the tank. "Be gentle," she said. "Don't frighten her."

Ali Baba took the tiny frog in his hands. Its body expanded and deflated as it breathed. Its eyes blinked.

"That's enough," said Valerie. "Put Farrah back in her home now."

"Just a minute," protested Ali Baba. He set the frog in the palm of his hand and examined its tiny legs. The skin was smoother than it looked in pictures of frogs. It was really a neat pet.

Suddenly Farrah gave a leap and, tiny though she was, she covered a huge distance. She landed on Valerie's bed. The bed was covered with a quilt that had a pattern of flowers. For a second, Farrah was sitting on a pink petal, but just as suddenly she jumped again. She must have landed on one of the green leaves because Ali Baba couldn't see her.

"If you don't find her, I'll hate you forever," Valerie threatened.

Ali Baba didn't particularly care what Valerie thought of him. But he didn't want the little frog to get lost.

"There she goes!" shouted Valerie.

"I got her," said Ali Baba, but he didn't.

"I got her," said Valerie, but she didn't, either.

The frog jumped onto the floor. The rug was pink so Farrah should have shown up well, but the pile was so deep and the frog was so small, it was hard to spot her except when she jumped straight into the air. On one of those leaps, Ali Baba managed to catch Farrah.

"Here," he said, handing the frog to Valerie. "She probably was dying to get some exercise."

"Oh, my darling," cooed Valerie, stroking the frog. "Were you afraid?"

"What was there for her to be afraid of?" asked Ali Baba. Girls are really silly, he thought.

Then he remembered a story he had once read. "Did you ever think that maybe Farrah isn't a frog at all?" he asked Valerie.

"Of course Farrah is a frog. Anyone with two eyes can see that," said Valerie.

"Oh, something can look like a frog," said Ali Baba, "if it has been enchanted into becoming a frog. But Farrah could be a prince."

"A prince?"

"Didn't you ever hear the story of the Frog Prince?" asked Ali Baba. "It's about a handsome prince who was turned into a frog by a wicked witch."

"Of course I know that story," said Valerie. "But Farrah is just a plain, ordinary frog. She's not a prince."

"Did you ever try?" asked Ali Baba.

"Try what?" asked Valerie.

"Kissing the frog."

Valerie stopped stroking her pet. "I couldn't kiss her," she said. "I might get germs or something."

"Then you'll never know," warned Ali Baba. "Farrah might really be a handsome prince. He might have looked like Christopher Reeve or John Travolta before the enchantment. And you never cared enough to find out. He might even die, and it will all be your fault."

Valerie looked very uncertain. "I found this frog on a trip to Bear Mountain. Suppose I hadn't found it. Then what?"

"Then some other girl would have found him," said Ali Baba. "And she probably would have kissed the frog on the very first night. Instead, he's had to sit in the dirt and eat bugs. If you love him, kiss him," said Ali Baba.

Slowly Valerie lifted the hand that was holding the frog closer to her face. She looked at the frog and frowned. "It can't be a prince. There isn't any more magic nowadays."

"Kiss the frog, Valerie," said Ali Baba.

Valerie took a deep breath. She brought her hand toward her mouth, and puckered her lips, and kissed the frog. Nothing happened.

"I made you kiss a frog!" Ali Baba said, grinning.

Valerie flushed.

"You should have seen your face," he said. "And you thought it would turn into a prince."

"No I didn't," Valerie protested. "I knew it wouldn't. It's a girl frog. It needs to be kissed by a boy. Then it will turn into a princess."

"Fat chance," said Ali Baba backing away.

"There's only one way to find out," said Valerie. She handed the frog to Ali Baba.

"Hey, that's my game," said Ali Baba.

"This is a female frog," said Valerie. "I took her to a pet shop and they told me. She's been waiting for a boy to kiss her and end the enchantment. My father couldn't do it because he's already married. You must break the spell for her."

"Come off it, Valerie," said Ali Baba. "Let's put the frog away and play one of your games."

"You want to sit and play a game while this poor princess is sitting in the dirt? You really are a mean person, Ali Baba. Luckily for Farrah, my cousin Lloyd is coming to visit next week. He's older than you and better looking, too. Farrah would prefer to be a princess for him and not for you, anyhow."

"How old is Lloyd?" asked Ali Baba.

"Ten. Practically eleven, actually," said Valerie.

Ali Baba thought for a moment. It couldn't hurt to kiss a frog. It might be an interesting experience. Why not? Gently his lips brushed Farrah's skin. Nothing happened. Ali Baba put her back inside the tank and rubbed his lips on his sleeve. At least Valerie didn't laugh, he noticed gratefully.

"My mother bought éclairs because you and your parents were coming," she said. "Do you want one?"

"Sure," said Ali Baba. He wanted to get away from all this kissing. Farrah stayed in the tank while Ali Baba and Valerie went into the kitchen. They each had a big, chocolate-covered, custard-filled pastry and a glass of milk.

"Have you ever thought of changing your name?" Ali Baba asked Valerie.

"Why should I?"

"Well," said Ali Baba, "don't you think it would be exciting to pick a new name for yourself? A special name that might help you have special adventures?"

"Like what?" asked Valerie.

"How about Sheherazade?" suggested Ali Baba. "Sheherazade Fishbone. It has a good ring to it."

Valerie grinned. "I like it," she said. "I bet I'd be the only person in any percentile with a name like that."

Ali Baba Bernstein and Sheherazade Fishbone finished eating their éclairs. Maybe it wasn't such a wasted afternoon after all.

5. ALI BABA AND THE KIDNAPPERS

O ne rainy Wednesday during the spring vacation from school, Ali Baba went to spend the afternoon with his friend Roger. Although he was glad to get out of his house, he was disappointed, too. Here he was eight years, ten months, and two days old, and nothing very exciting had happened to him yet.

"There should be a law against rain during

47

vacation," he told Roger as he removed his wet slicker and his rubber boots.

"BaBa, BaBa," Roger's little sister greeted him.

"Hiya Sugar," he said, smiling at the little girl. She was one of the few people who always remembered not to call him David.

Mrs. Zucker picked up her daughter. "It's time for your nap, Sugar."

"Come on," said Roger. "I want to show you the game I got for my new computer."

They had not been playing very long when Mrs. Zucker stuck her head in the door. "Boys," she said, "Sugar is in her crib. I'm going next door. Mrs. Kunkis is going to help me with this sweater that I'm knitting."

The boys nodded their heads, too absorbed in the commands of the computer game to pay much attention to what Mrs. Zucker was saying.

"I won't be long," said Mrs. Zucker. "Sugar shouldn't be any problem."

"Sure, Mom," said Roger.

"I'm leaving her door open in case she cries," said Mrs. Zucker.

Ali Baba listened. He could hear Sugar cooing contentedly from her crib. "RaRa, BaBa, MaMa." At sixteen months, she didn't know too many words.

Roger and Ali Baba went back to the game. It was called Kidnapped in the Castle. They had to give the computer commands to help them escape. But whenever the computer told them they had reached a door or a window, it was locked. And whenever they found a chest with a key inside, it was the wrong key. The kidnappers were hot on their trail.

Half an hour later, the boys had found four locked doors, two dead-end passages, three wrong keys, and the kidnappers were still on their trail. Mrs. Zucker had not returned from next door, and Sugar was fast asleep.

Ali Baba rubbed his eyes. He was getting tired from looking at the little green words on the monitor.

"I wish someone would come and kidnap us," he said.

"What do you mean?" asked Roger, who was pecking out the new command: KICK THE DOOR.

"People don't really get kidnapped. That only happens in the movies. It doesn't happen in real life."

Ali Baba disagreed. "I've heard about real kidnappings on TV."

"But we're not rich or famous," Roger said. "Nobody would want us."

"Someone could kidnap you and demand a million pounds of cheese."

"Speaking about cheese," said Roger, "do you want some Liederkranz?"

Ali Baba shook his head. He got up to stretch his legs. There was no sound from Sugar's room now. She must have fallen asleep. Ali Baba tiptoed to the open door of her room to peek in at the sleeping baby.

The crib was empty.

For a second, Ali Baba just stood there gaping. Where could Sugar be?

Ali Baba rushed back to Roger. His friend was still staring at the computer. "I think I found the right key this time," he said turning to look at Ali Baba.

"Where's Sugar?" asked Ali Baba.

"Where do you think? She's asleep in her crib."

"No she isn't," said Ali Baba. "I just looked there. The crib is empty."

"It can't be," said Roger. He rushed to his sister's room to check for himself.

"She's really gone!" Roger gasped.

"I told you," said Ali Baba. He got down on his hands and knees and looked under the crib. There was a stuffed rabbit and three blocks made out of foam rubber, but no baby.

"Listen," said Ali Baba. "I bet your mother took her next door and didn't tell us."

Roger ran to the phone and called Mrs. Kunkis. "This is Roger. Can I speak to my mother?"

"Don't tell her Sugar is missing," Ali Baba whispered.

"Hi, Mom," said Roger. "I just wanted to know how your knitting was going. No, Sugar isn't crying. No, she isn't doing anything at all. Okay," he said as he hung up the telephone.

"My mother said she'll be back in a little

while. Wait till she finds out that Sugar isn't here."

"She must have been kidnapped," said Ali Baba.

"I don't believe it," said Roger. "She has to be around here somewhere."

"What are we waiting for?" said Ali Baba. "Let's look for clues. If someone kidnapped Sugar, they would have left a ransom note."

"But how could someone get into the apartment? The door was locked. Besides, we would have heard them."

"Maybe they knew how to pick the lock. We were busy playing with the computer. If they put a gag on Sugar, we wouldn't have heard them at all."

Roger shook out Sugar's blanket. There was nothing under it.

"Don't touch the crib," Ali Baba warned his friend. "There may be fingerprints on it."

"Hey," whispered Roger. "If you're right, the kidnappers may still be in the apartment. Maybe they are planning to take you and me, too."

"They won't want me," Ali Baba whispered

back. I don't live here. They must have come for you and Sugar."

"But now that you're here, they'll take you, too," said Roger. "You'd be able to identify them to the police."

Ali Baba hadn't thought about that.

"Do you have any weapons?" asked Ali Baba.

"How about a baseball bat?"

"Perfect."

The boys tiptoed back to Roger's room. From the back of his closet he dug out a baseball bat and a tennis racket. "You can have this," he said, giving the tennis racket to Ali Baba.

Roger opened the bottom drawer of his dresser and grabbed an old cap pistol without any caps. He gave that to Ali Baba and took a water pistol for himself. "I'm going to fill this in the bathroom," he whispered to his friend.

Clinging tightly to the tennis racket, Ali Baba went into Roger's parents' bedroom. It was here that he had found the missing diamond. Maybe he would find Sugar here, too.

53

He looked around the room and saw nothing suspicious. The carpet cushioned his steps as he crept toward the closet. Holding the tennis racket above his head, he opened the closet door. It was a walk-in closet, so Ali Baba walked in. Something brushed his face. He stiffened, then realized that it was the light cord. He pulled the cord, and the closet was flooded with light. He could see Mr. and Mrs. Zucker's clothing hanging in neat rows. There were shoes resting in a shoe rack. But there was no little girl and no kidnapper in the closet. Ali Baba pulled the cord again and the light went out. He stepped out of the closet and felt a splash of water in his face.

"Where did you hide my sister?"

Ali Baba wiped his face with his shirt sleeve. "Oh," said Roger. "It's only you. I thought you were the kidnapper. I already looked in the bathroom and the kitchen."

Ali Baba went into the hall and opened the linen closet. Inside there were only towels and sheets.

Then they went into the living room. It was a large room. It would be easy for someone to

hide behind the couch. Ali Baba backed up and bumped into something. He was so startled he let go of the tennis racket.

"Ouch," said a voice. Ali Baba spun around.

"You dropped the tennis racket on my foot," Roger complained.

"We're even," said Ali Baba. "You squirted me with your water pistol."

"The kidnappers must have gotten away," said Roger.

"I guess they didn't want us," said Ali Baba. He felt a little left out.

"What will my mother say?" asked Roger. "She'll never let me watch Sugar again."

"You won't have to watch her anymore," said Ali Baba.

The boys sat down on the couch, side by side.

"She was a nice baby," Roger said. "She called me RaRa. Now she'll never learn to say Roger."

"She called me BaBa," Ali Baba said.

The boys sat together quietly, thinking of Roger's little sister.

Suddenly a sound broke the silence.

"There's someone else in the room with us," Roger whispered hoarsely.

Again they heard the sound.

"It's coming from behind the curtain," Ali Baba whispered to Roger. The floor-length living room curtains were drawn, covering the window. "Someone is hiding back there. You'd better go look."

"You go," Roger offered.

"It's your sister," said Ali Baba.

"Let's go together," Roger decided.

The boys stood clutching their weapons. Slowly they moved toward the curtains.

"You take that side, and I'll take the other," said Ali Baba. "We'll surround the kidnapper."

Reluctantly Roger moved away from Ali Baba.

Ali Baba lifted the tennis racket. Roger raised the baseball bat. Then Ali Baba's foot touched something soft. He jerked aside the curtain.

"It's Sugar!" Ali Baba shouted. "She escaped from the kidnapper."

Roger lowered the baseball bat and looked down on the floor. There, half-asleep and sucking her thumb, lay Sugar, safe and sound.

Roger grinned. "Once last week Sugar climbed out of her crib. I forgot all about it. She did it again. How about that? She wasn't kidnapped at all. She was here the whole time." He looked at Ali Baba. "I told you kidnappers wouldn't come here."

Ali Baba shrugged. He hated to admit it.

"I sure am glad she wasn't kidnapped," Roger said. "I don't know what we would have told my mother."

"Well," said Ali Baba. "In a way she was kidnapped. She kidnapped herself," he said.

Just then the boys heard a key in the lock.

"Do you think that's a kidnapper?" Ali Baba whispered to Roger.

"No. It's just my mother," said Roger, and he was right.

"What are you fellows doing?" asked Mrs. Zucker looking at the baseball bat and the tennis racket the boys were holding.

"It's a long story," said Ali Baba.

"But it has a happy ending," said Roger.

6. ALI BABA AND THE SNAIL SPELL

One morning when Ali Baba Bernstein was eight years, ten months, and four days old, he noticed a small bump on his right pinkie. He showed it to his mother.

"This looks like a wart," she said.

I bet I got it from Sheherazade Fishbone's frog, Ali Baba thought. He hoped he wasn't going to get a wart on his lips, too.

"It's nothing to worry about," said Mr.

Bernstein. "It will go away all by itself."

Ali Baba tried not to think about his wart. He had never paid much attention to his pinkie before. Suddenly he was always aware of it. The bump seemed to be getting bigger.

When he was writing something at school, his pinkie rubbed against the paper. When he sat watching television, Ali Baba would find himself picking on the dead skin around the wart. It was hard to stop himself. What had he done with his hands before he had the wart? He couldn't remember.

Mrs. Bernstein looked at Ali Baba's finger again. "It if doesn't go away soon, I'll take you to the doctor," she said. "He can remove it."

"Will it hurt?" Ali Baba asked.

"No, I'm sure it won't," his mother said.

But even with his mother's reassurance, Ali Baba was still worried about his wart. He remembered that he had held Farrah with both hands. Suppose one morning he woke up and his hands were totally covered with warts?

The next time Ali Baba was at the library, he looked up warts in a medical encyclopedia.

The book was almost as big as the Manhattan phone book, and it was filled with diagrams and charts and long difficult words. Under *W*, Ali Baba found the entry for warts. The book said warts were caused by a virus and often disappeared without treatment. It also said that there were many superstitions about warts. Some people thought they were caused by magic. Now that was an idea that Ali Baba liked. He decided right then and there to find a magic cure.

Ali Baba found a book on superstitions. It said that frogs and toads did not cause warts. "That shows you can't believe everything you read," Ali Baba said to himself. He had never had a wart in his life before he touched a frog. Then he had held Farrah, and within weeks, he had a wart on his finger. What more proof did he need?

He turned the page and read on. One method people had used for removing warts was to rub a grain of barley on it and then feed the barley to a chicken. When the barley disappeared down the chicken's gullet, it meant that the wart would disappear, too. Ali Baba

61

could not remember ever having seen a live chicken in Manhattan. Even the dead ones his mother brought home from the butcher no longer had their heads attached.

The next charm seemed more practical. You could rub a bean or a piece of stolen meat on the wart. Then the bean or meat had to be buried in the ground. As it decayed, the wart would dry up and disappear. That didn't sound too hard to arrange.

Luck was with Ali Baba. That very evening his mother served chicken cutlets and string beans for supper. They also had baked potatoes. The book hadn't mentioned potatoes at all, so Ali Baba was able to eat all of his. But when no one was looking, he slid a piece of chicken and one of the beans off his plate and into the napkin in his lap. As soon as supper was over, Ali Baba disappeared into his room with the napkin and its contents. He rubbed his wart with the chicken cutlet and the string bean. That was easy. It was also easy to bury them. There was a spider plant in his bedroom, and he just had to poke a little hole in the dirt. The only problem was that the book hadn't said what to do next. Would Ali Baba risk losing the good effects if he had to take a bath? He figured it would be better to skip washing that evening. At bedtime, he ran water in the bathroom sink so it sounded as if he was getting washed.

In the morning, the wart was the same, but Ali Baba's finger smelled slightly from the seasoned breadcrumbs, which had coated the chicken. Mrs. Bernstein said that Ali Baba looked a bit gray. "Be sure and wash yourself extra well this evening," she told him.

In school, Ali Baba finished his math quiz while the other students were still working. "Can I go to the library?" he asked Mrs. Booxbaum.

Mrs. Booxbaum smiled. "Certainly, David," she said.

"Ali Baba," he corrected his teacher. She almost never remembered his new name.

In the library, Ali Baba found another book about superstitions. This one had chants to recite. There was even one to say when rubbing a wart with a string bean:

As this bean shell rots away,
So my warts shall soon decay.

Drat. If only he had looked in this book yesterday he would have recited those words last night. Now they probably wouldn't even have string beans again for a week. He wondered if the chant would work with carrots or peas? Probably not, or the book would have mentioned it. Maybe he could dig up the bean he buried in the spider plant and reuse it.

Another chant went like this:

Ash tree, ashen tree,
Pray buy this wart of me.

Ali Baba had never seen an ash tree. All these chants for removing warts seemed to be for people living in the country. That was because frogs were in the country, too. He wondered how Sheherazade Fishbone was doing. By now, she might be covered with warts.

There was one more chant in the book:

Wart, wart on the snail's shell black
Go away soon and never come back.

You were supposed to rub a black snail on the wart while you were chanting. Too bad it was another country rhyme.

Ali Baba borrowed a piece of paper and a pencil from the librarian and copied all the verses. He folded the paper with the magic chants and put it into the pocket of his pants. Then he returned to the classroom.

As he sat down in his seat, he remembered the class aquarium. There was a snail in it that ate the algae growing on the glass walls of the tank. The snail's shell was black. Ali Baba could hardly sit still. He wanted to run right over to the tank.

The rest of the morning passed slowly. Ali Baba had no chance to get near the aquarium. When his class came back from lunch, Mrs. Booxbaum gave everyone ten minutes of free time to walk around the room or play quiet games. It was during this time of the day that the plant monitor watered the plants, the chalkboard monitors washed the boards, and the fish monitor fed the fish. Ali Baba hurried over to the fish tank. Every week a different student was fish monitor. In three weeks it would be Ali Baba's turn, but there was no way that he could wait that long. He wanted to cure his wart right now.

Roger Zucker was fish monitor this week. When Roger removed the cover from the top of the tank, Ali Baba stuck his hand inside and pulled out the snail. He reached in so quickly he didn't even think about rolling up his shirt sleeve first.

"Hey, what are you doing?" said Roger.

"I'm just borrowing the snail for a minute," said Ali Baba in a low voice. He didn't want the whole class to know.

"It will die out of the water," said Roger, trying to grab the snail away from Ali Baba.

A few kids wandered over to see what was happening. Fish feeding was usually a pretty dull activity. Today it looked a bit more interesting.

"Give me that snail," Roger hissed.

"I'll give it back," Ali Baba said. "I told you I would."

Roger grabbed Ali Baba's fist.

Ali Baba pushed Roger away.

Roger punched Ali Baba in the arm.

"Fight! Fight!" several kids called out. Before anyone could stop him, Ali Baba rushed out of the classroom clutching the snail in his right fist. He remembered to grab the wooden pass that you needed if you wanted to go to the boys' room. He would be safe there.

In the boys' room, Ali Baba closed himself inside one of the cubicles. He switched the snail to his left hand and took the paper with the rhymes out of his pocket. Rubbing the snail on his right pinkie, he chanted:

> *Wart, wart on the snail's shell black*
> *Go away soon and never come back.*

Just as he was finishing, he heard a sharp knock on the bathroom door.

"David, are you in there?"

It was Mrs. Booxbaum!

"I'll be right out," said Ali Baba rushing out of the cubicle. He did not bother to remind his teacher of his new name.

"Are you all right, David?" Mrs. Booxbaum called. "You know you aren't supposed to run out of the classroom without permission."

"I took the pass," Ali Baba called back.

"Roger says you took the snail out of the fish tank," said Mrs. Booxbaum to Ali Baba when he had come out.

"It's okay," said Ali Baba. "I'm going to put it right back."

"In our class we do not take snails out of the fish tank and bring them to the bathroom," said Mrs. Booxbaum sternly. "Where is the snail?"

Ali Baba opened his left hand and showed the snail to his teacher. "Put that snail back into the aquarium and go to your seat at once, David. I will have to speak to your parents about this."

All around him, Ali Baba's classmates were whispering. No one understood why he had taken the snail, and Ali Baba wasn't going to tell them. His wart was his business.

After supper that evening, Mrs. Bernstein got a phone call from Mrs. Booxbaum. When she had hung up, she called Ali Baba.

"What happened today in school?" she

asked. "Mrs. Booxbaum said you stole a snail out of the fish tank and were going to flush it down the toilet."

"That's a lie," said Ali Baba indignantly. "I told her I was going to put it right back into the aquarium."

"But why did you take it out?" asked Mrs. Bernstein.

"I had a private reason," said Ali Baba.

"You had better tell me all about it," said his mother. "Mrs. Booxbaum seems quite upset. She told me that you got into a fight with Roger, too."

"I didn't want to fight with Roger," Ali Baba protested. "But he was fish monitor, and he made a big deal when I took the snail out of the tank."

"Why this sudden interest in snails?" asked Mr. Bernstein, who had just come into the room.

"I only wanted to borrow the snail for a couple of seconds," said Ali Baba. "I needed it for the magic spell."

"What magic spell?" both parents exclaimed at once.

So Ali Baba had to explain how he had tried to cure his wart by rubbing it with the black snail shell and chanting. "It's too soon to tell," said Ali Baba. "But I bet I cured it now."

"I am going to take you to Dr. Clive tomorrow afternoon," said Mrs. Bernstein, putting her arm around Ali Baba. "He will know how to treat the wart properly. In the twentieth century, we don't have to rely on magic."

"But I like magic," said Ali Baba.

The next afternoon, Dr. Clive looked at Ali Baba's finger. "I diagnose an active imagination," said the doctor.

"How can that be treated?" asked Mrs. Bernstein.

"It is like the wart. It must be allowed to run its course."

"Are you sure?" asked Mrs. Bernstein.

"Quite," said Dr. Clive. "I had the same symptoms myself when I was young."

"What sort of things did you do when you were my age?" asked Ali Baba.

"No sense in my telling you," said the doctor. "You will think of enough things to do on your own."

So Mrs. Bernstein took Ali Baba home again. The wart remained for a long time, and Ali Baba forgot all about it. And one day when he suddenly remembered, it was gone.

"That's the way warts are," said Mr. Bernstein. "They just come and go."

But Ali Baba knew better. He believed in magic. As for Roger, in a couple of days the boys were good pals again. That had nothing to do with magic. That was friendship.

7. THE GATHERING OF DAVID BERNSTEINS

When Ali Baba Bernstein was eight years, eleven months, and four days old, his mother asked him how he wanted to celebrate his ninth birthday. He could take his friends to the bowling alley or to a movie. Or he could have a roller-skating party. None of these choices seemed very exciting to Ali Baba. Two boys in his class had already given bowling parties, another had invited all the boys in the class to a movie, and a third classmate was giving a roller-skating party next week. Ali Baba wanted to do something different.

"Do you remember when I counted all the David Bernsteins in the telephone book?"

Mrs. Bernstein nodded.

"I'd like to meet them all," said David. "I want to invite them here for my birthday."

"But you don't know them," his mother said. "And they are not your age."

"I want to see what they are all like," said Ali Baba. "If I can't invite them, then I don't want to have any party at all."

A week later, when Ali Baba was eight years, eleven months and twelve days old, his mother asked about his birthday again.

"I told you what I decided," said Ali Baba.

That night Ali Baba's parents talked about the David Bernstein party. Mr. Bernstein liked his son's idea. He thought the other David Bernsteins might be curious to meet one another. So it was agreed that Ali Baba would have the party he wanted.

The very next morning, which was Saturday, Ali Baba and his father went to his father's office. Ali Baba had written an invitation to the David Bernstein party.

Dear David Bernstein:

I found your name is the Manhattan telephone book. My name is David Bernstein, too. I want to meet all the David Bernsteins in New York. I am having a party on Friday, May 12th at 7:00 P.M., and I hope you can come.

My mother is cooking supper. She is a good cook.

Yours truly,
David Bernstein
(also known as Ali Baba Bernstein)
P.S. May 12th is my ninth birthday, but you don't have to bring a present. RSVP: 211-3579

Mr. Bernstein had explained that RSVP was a French abbreviation that meant please tell me if you are going to come. He also said that his son should give his age in the letter.

"Honesty is the best policy, Ali Baba," his father advised.

Ali Baba was going to use the word processor in his father's office to print the letter. It took him a long time to type his letter on the machine. His father tried to help him, but he did not type very well either. When the letter was finally completed and the print button pushed, the machine produced seventeen perfect copies—one for each David Bernstein.

That evening Ali Baba addressed the seventeen envelopes so that the invitations could be mailed on Monday morning. His father supplied the stamps. By the end of the week, two David Bernsteins had already called to accept.

By the time Ali Baba Bernstein was eight years, eleven months, and twenty nine days old, seven David Bernsteins had accepted his invitation. Four David Bernsteins called to say they couldn't come.

Six David Bernsteins did not answer at all.

Ali Baba and his mother chose the menu for his birthday dinner. There would be pot roast, corn (Ali Baba's favorite vegetable), rolls, applesauce, and salad. They were also having kasha varnishkas (a combination of buckwheat groats and noodles), which one of the guests had requested.

The evening of the party finally arrived. Ali Baba had decided to wear a pair of slacks, a sport jacket, and real dress shoes. It was not at all the way he would have dressed for a bowling party.

Ali Baba was surprised when the first guest arrived in a jogging suit and running shoes.

"How do you do," he said when Ali Baba opened the door. "I'm David Bernstein."

"Of course," said the birthday boy. "Call me Ali Baba."

Soon the living room was filled with David Bernsteins. They ranged in age from exactly nine years and three hours old to seventy-six years old (he was the David Bernstein who had asked for kasha varnishkas). There was a television director, a delicatessen owner, a mailman, an animal groomer, a dentist, a high-school teacher, and a writer. They all lived in Manhattan now, but they had been born in Brooklyn, the Bronx, Michigan, Poland, Germany, and South Africa. None of them had ever met any of the others before.

All of the guests enjoyed the dinner.

"David, will you please pass those delicious rolls," asked the mailman.

"Certainly, David," said the animal groomer on his left.

"David, would you please pass the pitcher of apple cider this way," asked the dentist.

"Here it is, David," said the television director.

"I have trouble remembering names," the seventy-six-year-old David Bernstein told Ali Baba. "At this party I can't possibly forget." He smiled at Ali Baba. "What did you say your nickname was?"

"Ali Baba is not a nickname. I have chosen it to be my real name. There are too many David Bernsteins. There were even more in the telephone book who didn't come tonight."

"I was the only David Bernstein to finish the New York City Marathon," said David Bernstein the dentist. He was the one wearing running shoes.

"The poodles I clip don't care what my name is," said David Bernstein the animal groomer.

"It's not what you're called but what you do that matters," said the seventy-six-year-old David Bernstein.

All of them agreed to that.

"I once read that in some places children are given temporary names. They call them 'milk names.' They can then choose whatever names they want when they get older," said David Bernstein the high-school teacher.

"I'd still choose David Bernstein," said David Bernstein the delicatessen owner. "Just because we all have the same name doesn't make us the same."

"You're right," agreed David Bernstein the mailman.

"Here, here," called out David Bernstein the television director. He raised his glass of apple cider. "A toast to the youngest David Bernstein in the room."

Everyone turned to Ali Baba. He was about to say that he didn't want to be called David. But somehow he didn't mind his name so much now that he had met all these other David Bernsteins. They *were* all different. There would never be another David Bernstein like himself. One of these days he might go back to calling himself David again. But not just now.

"Open your presents," called out David Bernstein the writer.

Even though he had said that they didn't have to, several guests had brought gifts. So after singing "Happy Birthday" and cutting into the ice-cream cake that was shaped like the Manhattan phone book, Ali Baba began to open the packages. There was a pocket calculator the size of a business card, just like the one his father had. There was a jigsaw puzzle that looked like a subway map of Manhattan, a model airplane kit, and a few books. One was a collection of Sherlock Holmes stories. "I used to call myself Sherlock Bernstein," the high-school teacher recalled. There was an atlas, and, best of all, there was *The Arabian Nights*.

"Now I have my own copy!" said Ali Baba. This was the best birthday he had ever had.

Finally, it was time for the guests to leave. "I never thought I would meet all the David Bernsteins," said David Bernstein the writer.

"You haven't," said Ali Baba. "Besides the seventeen David Bernsteins in the telephone book, there are six hundred eighty-three other Bernsteins listed between Aaron Bernstein and Zachary Bernstein. There must be members of their families who are named David. I bet there are thousands of David Bernsteins that I haven't met yet."

"You're right," said the seventy-six-year-old David Bernstein, patting Ali Baba on the back.

"Maybe I could invite them all next year," said Ali Baba. He was already nine years and six hours old.

"You could put an advertisement in the newspaper," suggested the mailman.

Ali Baba liked that idea.

David Bernstein the writer said, "I just might go home and write all about this. When did you get so interested in all the David Bernsteins?"

"It goes back a long time," said Ali Baba. "It all started on the day that I was eight years, five months, and seventeen days old."

JOHANNA HURWITZ

grew up in New York and received degrees from Queens College and Columbia University. She has worked as a children's librarian in many school and public libraries in both New Yory City and Long Island. Her humorous stories about Aldo, Nora and Teddy, and various other characters have made friends for her throughout the United States. In addition, several of her books have been published abroad in translation. Ms. Hurwitz lives in Great Neck, New York with one husband, two children, and two cats.

GAIL OWENS

is a well-known children's book artist living and working in Rock Tavern, New York. Among the many books she has illustrated are *Angie's First Case* by Donald J. Sobol and *The Hot & Cold Summer* by Johanna Hurwitz.

W9-ATS-922

FAT MEN
FROM SPACE

OTHER YEARLING BOOKS YOU WILL ENJOY:

CHOCOLATE FEVER, *Robert Kimmel Smith*
JELLY BELLY, *Robert Kimmel Smith*
THE BOX OF DELIGHTS, *John Masefield*
A WRINKLE IN TIME, *Madeleine L'Engle*
A WIND IN THE DOOR, *Madeleine L'Engle*
A SWIFTLY TILTING PLANET, *Madeleine L'Engle*
TIME CAT, *Lloyd Alexander*

YEARLING BOOKS/YOUNG YEARLINGS/YEARLING CLASSICS are designed especially to entertain and enlighten young people. Patricia Reilly Giff, consultant to this series, received her bachelor's degree from Marymount College. She holds a master's degree in history from St. John's University, and a Professional Diploma in Reading from Hofstra University. She was a teacher and reading consultant for many years, and is the author of numerous books for young readers.

For a complete listing of all Yearling titles,
write to Dell Readers Service,
P.O. Box 1045, South Holland, IL 60473.

FAT MEN
FROM SPACE

Written and illustrated by

DANIEL MANUS PINKWATER

A YEARLING BOOK

Published by
Dell Publishing Co., Inc.
1 Dag Hammarskjold Plaza
New York, New York 10017

Copyright © 1977 by Manus Pinkwater

All rights reserved. No part of this book may be reproduced in any form without permission in writing from the publisher. For information address Dodd, Mead & Company, New York, New York.

Yearling® TM 913705, Dell Publishing Co., Inc.

ISBN: 0-440-44542-6

Reprinted by arrangement with Dodd, Mead & Company

Printed in the United States of America

August 1980

10 9 8

CW

TO S. KILNISAN

(the biggest baby ever born in Budapest)

FAT MEN
FROM SPACE

William went to the dentist. It wasn't so bad—just a filling. The dentist said it wouldn't hurt a bit, and it was almost true. William went home feeling a little bit numb. There was a funny sour taste in his mouth that made him think of electricity. When he sucked in his breath, the tooth with the new filling felt cold. He was able to eat his supper without any trouble, and after watching television with his mother and father, he went to bed.

One of the things William liked to do in bed, and wasn't allowed to, was listen to the radio. William thought that if he had a little radio, with an earphone, he could listen in bed without bothering anybody. He mentioned this to his parents, and found out that not bothering anybody wasn't the point. "I don't want you listening to the radio when you should be sleeping," his mother said. Sometimes William would turn on the radio on the table near his bed, very softly, and try to listen. Usually, his mother would hear it, and tell him to turn it off.

This particular night, after William had been to the

dentist, he was lying in bed listening to the radio. He was listening to a talk show. A man who said he had taken a ride in a flying saucer was telling how the people from outer space were crazy about potato pancakes, and had come to Earth in search of millions of them, which they planned to freeze and take back to their own galaxy. It was a good show, and William was enjoying it. He was ready to drift off to sleep, when he realized that he had never turned the radio on. He checked this. He clicked on the radio next to his bed. It was tuned to a music station. He could still hear the man talking about the flying saucers, over the music. "Are you playing the radio?" his mother shouted from down the hall.

William turned off the radio. The flying-saucer man was still talking. "Can you hear the radio now?" he asked.

"No. Don't turn it on again," his mother said.

His mother could not hear the man talking about the flying saucers. Where was it coming from? William lay very quietly, trying to figure out where the radio program was coming from. It seemed to be coming from inside his head. "Maybe I'm imagining the whole thing," he thought. "Maybe I'm going crazy." It seemed like an ordinary radio program—there wasn't anything crazy about it. He had heard the same talk show before. The

8

announcer was telling people to buy the same bottled spring water, and canned hams, and pianos that always sponsored the program. It was a real radio program going on inside William's head. It worried him. He rubbed the tip of his tongue against the new filling. The volume dropped very low. Wait a second! He did it again. The volume dropped. He pressed his tongue against the tooth. No radio program at all! It was the tooth! The one with the new filling was receiving radio programs! William clenched his teeth. The volume got louder.

"I told you to turn that off!" his mother shouted.

William got up. He went quietly out into the backyard. He clenched his teeth. The radio got louder. He clenched them harder. It got louder still. Keeping his teeth clenched, he pulled his lips back in a big grin. It got so loud that it made an echo. He could hear windows opening, and people shouting, "Turn that thing down!"

"... AND THEN THE CAPTAIN OF THE SPACECRAFT ASKED ME IF I KNEW WHERE THERE WERE A LOT OF POTATO PANCAKES," the radio tooth said. William jumped up and down. This was wonderful. He didn't know how it worked, but it was wonderful. He had a built-in radio.

William scurried back to bed before anyone could call

the cops. He had waked up the whole neighborhood. He was barely able to lie still, he was so excited about his built-in radio. He decided it would be the most fun if he didn't tell anybody about it for a while. Finally, he got tired of planning ways to use his radio tooth, and bored listening to the man talking about flying saucers and potato pancakes. He put his tongue over his tooth and went to sleep.

At breakfast, when William put a spoonful of cornflakes into his mouth, the spoon touched the tooth and changed the station. It had been playing news, but it changed to rock and roll. William took the spoon out—news. He put the spoon back—rock and roll. He tried a fork—news and country and western music at the same time. He put a butter knife into his mouth—classical music.

"William, will you stop playing with the silverware," his father said, "and I think someone left a radio playing upstairs." William put his tongue over his tooth. It wasn't easy to finish breakfast and keep the radio from playing.

At school, William resisted the temptation to use his radio tooth to show off. There were a lot of kids standing around in the schoolyard, waiting for the bell to ring. William stayed by himself, chewing on the wire binding of

his spiral notebook. Depending on where he bit into the wire, he could get different stations.

Mr. Wendel was William's teacher. He didn't stand for any nonsense, and because he was hard to fool, the kids tried to trick him all the time. Nobody ever succeeded. Kids were always planning to put glue on his chair, or substitute fake chalk made of soap. When these things were tried, Mr. Wendel always spotted the glue or the fake chalk, and turned the joke around by asking one of the kids to sit in his chair or write on the blackboard. Usually, he picked the kid who had thought of the trick in the first place.

Lots of kids in Mr. Wendel's class had sent away at one time or another for a book on how to throw your voice. The book came with a little device to hold in your mouth, that was supposed to make it easy to throw your voice. The kids who didn't actually swallow the little voice-throwers had them taken away by Mr. Wendel. It was hard to fool Mr. Wendel.

Other kids had read a book on mind power, and tried to hypnotize Mr. Wendel by staring at him and repeating silently, "Mr. Wendel, you are my slave. . . . My will is stronger." Mr. Wendel's will was stronger—and the kids who had tried to hypnotize him wound up with a new seat near the front of the room, and a note to their parents suggesting an eye examination.

In the classroom, William clenched his teeth. *". . . and then you add the graham crackers to the heated chicken fat. Add paprika, salt, and pepper . . ."* It was a cooking program. All the kids giggled and looked around to see where the noise was coming from. William looked around too. Mr. Wendel didn't say anything. *"Garnish with banana slices in their skin. This festive dish will serve four . . ."* Mr. Wendel walked up and down the aisles, trying to locate the sound. As Mr. Wendel got closer, William unclenched his teeth little by little, so that the sound of the radio got softer. As Mr. Wendel got farther away, he clenched his teeth gradually, so that the sound got louder. He was trying to control the volume so that it seemed to remain constant to Mr. Wendel, wherever he was. Mr. Wendel stopped. William put his tongue over his tooth.

"Melvyn, give me the radio," Mr. Wendel said. He had picked on Melvyn Schwartz—the wrong kid! Nobody knew that he had picked wrong, except William, and Melvyn Schwartz. Mr. Wendel had never picked wrong before. Melvyn was delighted.

"Aw, geez, Mr. Wendel, it isn't fair. You always pick on me," Melvyn said. He was just warming up. "I demand my constitutional rights. You have no reason to accuse me. I demand a trial by a jury of my peers."

"You are peerless, Melvyn," Mr. Wendel said. "Give me the radio."

"I protest," Melvyn said, rising from his desk. "You are persecuting me because of my past misfortunes." Melvyn was the one who had put glue on Mr. Wendel's chair. "I want a lawyer!"

"You will have the best defense that money can buy," Mr. Wendel said. "After that—Devil's Island. Give me the radio."

"I have no radio," Melvyn said, trying to look shifty-eyed and guilty. The class was enjoying this. It was obvious to them that Melvyn was having a lot of fun.

"Melvyn, open your desk," Mr. Wendel said.

"I demand to see your search warrant," Melvyn said.

"Our principal, Mr. Feeney, will be glad to listen to your complaint about illegal search," Mr. Wendel said. "Now, open your desk."

"Storm trooper," Melvyn said, and opened his desk. It was empty, except for Melvyn's history book. "Didn't I tell

14

you?'' Melvyn made a sweeping gesture to the class, which burst into loud applause.

William clenched his teeth, just a little. The radio played faintly.

"Melvyn, empty your pockets," Mr. Wendel said. Melvyn emptied his pockets and turned them inside out. No radio. He smiled broadly at Mr. Wendel.

"Melvyn, I apologize for having suspected you," Mr. Wendel said.

"I'll never trust anyone in authority again," Melvyn said.

William was clenching as hard as he could to get the volume high enough to be heard over the applause and laughter. Melvyn was taking bows from his seat.

"All right, who's got the radio?" Mr. Wendel asked. A mistake—Mr. Wendel was stumped, and he had shown it. The celebration got louder and louder. "I'm going to step outside the room for a minute, and when I come back, I want everybody to be quiet and I want the radio to have stopped playing," Mr. Wendel said. A miserable trick—it sometimes worked for old lady teachers—the class would think they were crying in the hall, and lay off out of sympathy. It didn't work for Mr. Wendel.

16

When he came back, an announcer was saying, *"In Chicago a kangaroo is still loose in the streets ... "*

Mr. Wendel was beaten. He fell back on another old tactic. "You are all suspended. You will leave school at once, and not come back until tomorrow *with* a note from your parents."

The idea of a day off from school as a punishment didn't fool anyone. The kids all said "Aww, fooey," and "it isn't fair," as they were expected to, but in their hearts they were thanking the kid with the radio, whoever it was.

A group punishment was easy to explain at home. Every kid's parents would automatically assume that some other kid, and not their little darling, had caused the disturbance.

On the way home with the other kids, William kept his tongue over his tooth and said nothing. Later, he planned to claim credit for the great thing he had done, but for now he was going to enjoy his tooth in secret.

It never occurred to William's mother to ask if William had been one of the kids who misbehaved and got the whole class sent home. She went to the market, leaving William alone with his tooth. He was getting curious about it. Had the dentist put a little radio inside his tooth? Why would he do such a thing?

The dentist was a pretty nice guy. Maybe if William called him up and asked him . . . William looked up the dentist in his mother's little leather telephone book. Dr. Horwitz. He dialed the number. Dr. Horwitz answered. "This is William Pedwee," William said. "Can you tell me something about the tooth you filled for me yesterday?"

"I'll tell you if I can," Dr. Horwitz said.

"What I'd like to know is, why is my tooth receiving radio programs?"

"Your tooth is receiving radio programs? No kidding?" Dr. Horwitz sounded interested.

"Yes, it is," William said. "Did you put a little radio in my tooth?"

"I may have," Dr. Horwitz said, "but it wasn't on purpose. Sometimes when we put a metal filling in a tooth, it reacts with a different kind of metal in another filling. It makes an electric current. It is just possible that a filling could have the properties of a radio receiver, or an old-fashioned crystal set. This isn't a joke, is it, William?"

William told Dr. Horwitz that he was not joking. He gritted his teeth, and Dr. Horwitz heard, *"Tonight at the civic wrestling arena . . . the Human Ape versus Doctor Death! Be sure to see this great match."*

"Was that the tooth?" Dr. Horwitz asked.

"That was it," William said.

"Well, well," Dr. Horwitz said, "I've heard of this happening—once in a million fillings—but it has never happened to me. Tell you what—come right over, and we'll put a coating over that filling, and get rid of those radio programs for you."

"Get rid of them?" William shouted. "Are you kidding? I like my tooth!"

"Oh, you like it, do you?" said Dr. Horwitz. "You just wanted some information. Well, enjoy your tooth, William. If you ever get tired of it, come see me, and we'll fix it up."

William thanked Dr. Horwitz and said good-by.

He was happier than ever about his radio tooth. One in a million, it was. William felt that he was a special person to have such a special tooth.

"And now the number-one tune on the charts, I'll Never Forget Your Nose." William listened to the music as he fished around in his dresser drawer for something to use as an antenna. He found a coil of wire that had come out of an old doorbell he had taken apart. He unwound a few

feet of wire and clamped the end between his teeth. *"And that's the local news in the Trinidad, Colorado, area."* William knew he wasn't anywhere *near* Colorado. He listened to the station—sure enough, it was a radio station in Trinidad, Colorado. He let go of the wire, and the station switched back to the familiar local one. *". . . and tonight be sure to tune in when Barry Garble talks to a man who has lived underwater for the past fifteen years."*

William thought of another trick to play with his tooth radio. He had just heard the back door slam. His mother was home from the market. William went downstairs to see her. There was a radio in the kitchen. To turn it on, you pushed a button. To turn it off, you pushed the same button again. William helped his mother put away the groceries. Then he asked her for a cookie and a glass of milk.

While his mother was getting a cookie, William clenched his teeth. *"The President has a cold today, and did not come to work,"* the tooth radio said.

William's mother reached up and pushed the button to turn off the kitchen radio, which turned it on. *"Are you tired? Depressed? Miserable? Stupid? Klunkie's Pills,*

21

made with real extract of chopped chicken livers, will—"

She pushed the button again. William clenched his teeth. *"The President's physician said that the President should get plenty of rest, drink liquids, and stay out of drafts."*

William's mother was getting annoyed. She pushed the button again hard. William unclenched his teeth. The kitchen radio came on. *"Klunkie's Pills cure asthma, chills, fever, and—"*

She pushed the button so hard that the radio almost fell off the shelf. William clenched his teeth. *"Back in 1957, President Eisenhower had a cold—"*

She pushed the button. She was getting red in the face. *". . . malaria, mange, baldness, pimples, thrips—"*

William's mother pulled the plug. "What is wrong with this radio?" she said. "I'll have your father look at it when he gets home."

William was almost choking on the cookie. He was having a hard time not laughing. Before he left the room, he clenched his teeth for a couple of seconds. *"President Coolidge had a cold in . . ."* William's mother looked at the dangling plug. William had to run upstairs so she wouldn't hear him laughing.

When William's father came home, he spent a lot of time whispering in the kitchen with William's mother. That wasn't usual, but William didn't pay any special attention to it. At the supper table he noticed that his parents were smiling and winking at each other quite a lot. He thought they must be in an extra good mood.

"Something is wrong with the kitchen radio," William's mother said. William waited, and listened to the radio station inside his head. A station break was coming. He clenched. *"This is WXXO Radio—"*

"Did someone say radio?" William's father asked.

William clenched. *". . . radio all day and all night—"*

"Have some carrots," William's mother said.

William clenched his teeth as hard as he could. *"AND NOW THE NEWS. TODAY A LARGE CARDBOARD CARTON OF FROZEN POTATO PANCAKES WAS SIGHTED FLOATING IN OUTER SPACE—"*

"Do you want some more milk, William?" his mother said.

What was wrong? Why couldn't his parents hear the radio? William had been clenching his teeth as hard as he could. The radio tooth was so loud It almost gave him a headache.

"You'll never guess who I met downtown today," William's father said. "It was Dr. Horwitz, the dentist who takes care of William's teeth."

"He's an awfully nice man," William's mother said. She was starting to giggle.

"Yes he is," William's father said, "a very nice man, and so interesting. He told me some fascinating things about dentistry."

So that was it. Horwitz had finked. William decided that he was going to bite Dr. Horwitz's finger one of these days.

"And guess who happened to come by while we were talking," William's father went on.

"Who was it, dear?" William's mother was laughing so hard she could hardly talk.

"It was Mr. Wendel, William's teacher," his father said, "and *he* had something fascinating to tell us. It seems that someone in William's class was playing a radio today, and Mr. Wendel just couldn't find it. The poor man finally had to send the whole class home."

"That certainly is fascinating," William's mother said. She was laughing so hard now that she had to hang onto the table to keep from falling out of her chair. "And what did Dr. Horwitz have to say about dentistry that was so fascinating?"

"It seems that Dr. Horwitz had just done a filling for one of his patients, and that filling turned out to work just like a radio."

"Imagine that," William's mother said. "Was the patient anyone we know?"

"Now, let me think," his father said. "I believe it was someone we know. Now who was it? Oh, yes! It was our very own son, William!"

William's father and mother were both helpless with laughter. He hated it when they got this way. He was good and mad. Why did Dr. Horwitz have to go blabbing things? And why did Mr. Wendel have to turn up, and make things worse? Some day he was going to get even with those guys.

William's parents were finished laughing, and were now at the wet-eyed and sighing stage. William got ready for the serious part.

"William, Mr. Wendel understands that there will be no more problems with radios in school," his father said, "and Dr. Horwitz is of the opinion that your tooth will settle down in a day or two and stop receiving—but if it doesn't, he can see you on Saturday and put a nice coating of epoxy on it. Meanwhile, no more tricks, and no listening to your tooth in bed. Now, see if you can get me the baseball scores on your molar, son.'' At this point, William's father collapsed into laughter again. William got up and walked straight out of the kitchen, into the backyard. He was disgusted. Adults never know a good thing when they see it. His tooth was one in a million, and his parents thought it was a big joke.

William stood in the backyard. He could hear his parents laughing inside the house. They thought the whole thing was funny. They didn't care that they had just ruined everything for their only son. William was angry and miserable. It wasn't going to be very much fun, having a one-in-a-million tooth, if it was going to be coated with epoxy in a few days. ''If I ever have a little boy, and he is lucky enough to get a radio tooth, I'm going to do everything I can to help him enjoy it,'' William thought.

William fished the piece of wire, the part of a taken-apart doorbell, out of his pocket. He played with the wire, idly, while standing in the backyard. It was a heavy, damp night. There was a storm brewing somewhere. Already, William could see a little glow in the sky now and then—lightning a long way off. He put one end of the wire in his

26

mouth. *"In East Trinidad, there will be a meeting of the Cowboy's Mah Jong Club, behind the feed store at seven-thirty."* It was that station in Trinidad, Colorado. It was coming in very clear. William remembered that he had planned to try out a longer piece of wire. He had some up in his room, but he didn't want to go back into the house. He didn't want to see his mother and father. He was still mad at them. Then William had a bright idea.

All around the backyard was a metal chain-link fence. William could wrap one end of his piece of wire around a fence post, and the whole thing would act as one immense antenna. He cheered up. "I bet I get to hear China," he said.

William twisted one end of his wire around a fence post. The other end he put in his mouth. Then he had a very unusual experience. He felt a thumping—like the thumping of a bass drum—and he heard a sort of rushing, buzzing noise. And he saw amazing colors, purple and red and blue. And his body did things all by itself. All these things seemed to be going on for a long time, but William knew they were happening very fast. And while all those things were happening, William was remembering all he knew about static electricity. He thought about when it is cold and dry, and you rub your feet on the carpet—and

you touch the doorknob, and there is a snap, and you can see a little spark. It seemed to William that the chain-link fence had stored up a very big charge of static electricity, and William had bitten right into it. He noticed that he was lying in the grass and having a hard time catching his breath. Nothing hurt him, but he had a very funny taste in his mouth.

Then William noticed that his tooth was not receiving. At first, he thought the tooth had gone completely dead. Then he was able to hear some faint static. But there was no program. There was no WXXO. William clenched his teeth. The static got louder. William listened. He was lying in the grass, where he had landed when he got the shock. The static was kind of rhythmical, like music. It was interesting. William thought it was almost like a language.

The more William listened to the strange static, the more he felt that he could almost understand it. It wasn't as though he could hear words coming through the crackling and whistling. It was the noise itself that had meaning. When William tried to listen hard, it was difficult to understand. When he just relaxed, and half-paid attention, it was almost possible to understand.

"William, we're going now. We'll be visiting across the

street. Don't lie there in the grass all evening." It was William's parents. A few months ago, there had been some big arguments about baby-sitters. William had finally persuaded his parents that he was old enough to be left by himself, at least when they were not going any farther away than the house of a neighbor across the street.

"I'll go in soon," William said. "I'm just looking at the sky." He was not exactly lying. He was looking at the sky, while listening to the strange rhythmic static on his tooth. It looked as though it might not rain after all. The clouds were breaking up, and a few stars were showing.

The static was starting to make sense. It wasn't like anything William had ever heard. He knew what the noises meant. He could tell the directions they came from. The noises were spacemen talking to one another.

Somehow, William's tooth had been converted to receive the signals between the spacemen. Probably the charge of static electricity had done it. The static told William more than words ever did. He could tell that there were a number of different spacemen talking. Some were far away in spaceships, some were on the Earth. William could tell where the spacemen were in relation to one another. He could tell how fast they were moving, and in which direction. It was almost as if he could see the spaceships. It was like listening to a baseball game on the radio. He could see the players in their various positions. As new information came over the radio, William could move the players in his mind—play the game in his mind.

This was better than a baseball game. The field was thousands of miles—millions of miles. The players were spaceships that moved with such speed, they could go so fast and so far, that they would disappear in seconds and reappear in some other part of the sky. They reminded William of those bugs that scoot on the surface of water in summer.

William was listening to twenty or thirty conversations at once. He had no trouble sorting them out. He could tell where each spaceman was, and what he was talking about. Some of the conversations were about potato pancakes. Some spacemen were assembling huge piles of potato pancakes in remote places on Earth. Spaceships would come and collect the potato pancakes and speed away with them. Other conversations were about navigation, and spaceships keeping in touch with one another. Some of the conversations were about a boy, an

31

earth-boy who was listening in. The spacemen knew that William was listening! It made him shiver.

One of the spaceships was getting closer! As it got closer, the static from the spaceship got louder and clearer. It seemed to William that the spaceship was getting bigger and bigger. It was zooming toward him. William decided to get up and go inside the house. He discovered that he couldn't move. He couldn't even twitch a finger. He could see the spaceship—a spot of light, a long way off. It was getting bigger and bigger. He could see it clearly. It was saucer-shaped, and glowing and spinning. The static from the spaceship was so loud that William couldn't even hear his heart, which was pounding. Now the spaceship was directly over him, and falling. He was sure the thing was going to crush him. The static kept telling him not to be scared, but he was scared anyway. He was good and scared.

The saucer stopped falling, and just hung in the air, about twenty feet above him. William could see that it was made of metal. It had a reddish color, that changed to blue or green from time to time. It was spinning slowly, and rocking slightly from side to side. Up till now, William had not thought of screaming for help. He thought of it

now, and gave it a try. The static was so loud that he couldn't tell if anything was getting out.

He was still screaming, or trying to, when he started floating up. He was moving through the air slowly, as though something were drawing him up toward the spaceship, and he was spinning with the spaceship. It was a weird feeling. William didn't like it. It must have taken about a minute for William to spin and float up to the saucer. When he had almost reached it, a hole appeared in the metal skin of the thing. It wasn't like a door; it was a round hole that appeared in the metal, very small, and got larger as William got closer. As he passed through it, the hole closed again under him. He knew this because he found himself lying on a solid metal floor the moment he had gone through.

All around him were cardboard cartons. They were ordinary cartons, the kind that pile up behind the supermarket. They had advertising for cigarettes and toilet tissues printed on them. They were all different sizes and shapes, and they were all full of potato pancakes, fresh and frozen.

William discovered he could move again. He had a look at the room he was in. It was glowing with a greenish light that seemed to come from everywhere. The walls and floor and ceiling were made of metal. There was a little round thing on the ceiling, made of shiny metal. It was about the size of a tennis ball, and covered with little bumps. The room seemed to be a sort of storage room or closet.

"You have been captured by a spaceburger from the planet Spiegel." It was the little round thing talking—a sort of loudspeaker. It was making the same sort of static noise that William had been receiving on his tooth. He understood it perfectly. "No harm will come to you. You will be treated fairly, and returned to your home," the speaker went on. William was good and scared, even though the little round metal thing had told him that no harm would come to him.

"I want to go home," William said.

"That is not possible at this time," the speaker said, "but we will let you out of the storage hold."

"Fine," William said, "let me out."

"First you must promise that you will not attempt to harm the spaceburger, and that you will abide by the regulations governing spacemen on board this craft."

"I promise," William said.

"Also you must promise not to tell anyone about the things you see and hear on the spaceburger," the speaker said.

"I won't say a word," William said.

"In a few seconds a door will open, and you may go up the ladder," the speaker said.

William was a little scared at the thought of meeting the spacemen. He had seen a lot of science-fiction movies. Maybe they were green and scaly, like lizards. Maybe they had heads like flies, with big weird fly-eyes. Maybe they were like green weeds, and talked in horrible whispers.

There was nothing to do but go and find out. A door opened—it just appeared in the wall, like the round hole William had floated through when he had been brought on board, and beyond it a ladder. William climbed the ladder. The ladder took him up into a metal corridor. It was glowing green like the storage hold, only brighter. It was hot in the corridor, and William could hear something buzzing. He had an idea that he was somewhere near the engine, or whatever made the spaceburger go.

William walked along the corridor until he came to the end. There weren't any doors, just smooth metal walls, glowing green. At the end of the corridor was another
36

round shiny metal speaker, like the one in the storage hold. "Are you out there?" the speaker said.

"Yes," William said. A door appeared, and William stepped into a room. He could tell it was the control room of the spaceburger. It looked like the control room of all the spaceships he had seen in movies, and on TV. There were lots of TV screens and flashing lights, and panels of buttons and dials. There was also a deep-fryer and a soft ice cream machine.

The spacemen weren't at all what William had expected. They looked like ordinary earth-people, except that they were fatter than most. William guessed that they weighed at least 350 pounds apiece. There were seven or eight of them. They didn't have the sort of uniforms that William had always seen spacemen wearing in movies. All the spacemen were wearing plaid sport jackets, and dacron slacks. They had knitted neckties, and black-and-white shoes with thick rubber soles. They all had crew cuts and they all wore eyeglasses made of heavy black plastic. The only thing about their clothing that was sort of nifty and spacemanlike was their belts. The belts were wide and made out of white plastic. They had silver buckles in the shape of a cheeseburger with a bolt of lightning going through it. Some of the spacemen had tie clips with the same design.

"I am Hanam, the Captain of this spaceburger," one of the spacemen said. "We apologize for having to capture you, but we had a bad experience not long ago. It seems one of our spaceburgers picked up an earth person, and, even though he promised not to say anything about it, as soon as he was released, he went on a radio program and blabbed about everything he had seen. We can't take the chance that you'll do the same thing—especially now, so close to the invasion."

"Invasion?" William said. "Are you going to invade Earth?"

"Of course we are," Hanam said. "Don't you ever go to the movies? Spacemen always invade places. We have been collecting all the potato pancakes we can find and shipping them back to our leader, Sargon, on the planet Spiegel—they're his favorite. Now that we have collected most of the potato pancakes, we are getting ready to invade."

"But why do you want to invade Earth?" William asked. "We never did anything to hurt you."

"Because we are pirates," Hanam said, "space pirates.

38

All we do is invade planets and take whatever we want. Then we go back to Spiegel, and have big celebrations. After a while, we go out and invade some more planets. It's a lot of fun."

"There aren't very many of you," William said.

"Oh, there are very many of us, all right." Hanam said. "This is just a potato-pancake collecting ship. The main fleet will be arriving any time now. Then the fun begins."

William was very worried by the things Hanam was saying. He was afraid the spacemen would hurt his mother and father. He had seen movies in which spacemen came to Earth with death rays and things that shot fire and turned people to mush. "Do you have death rays?" William asked, "Are you going to knock down all the tall buildings in Tokyo and Los Angeles?"

"Mercy, no," Hanam said. "We don't do anything nasty like that. All we do when we invade a planet is walk around and have a snack, and we don't pay for it either. After a while we use up all the things we came to get, and then we enslave the local population, and get them to produce more of the things we like. That's all. We don't do anything destructive."

Hanam seemed very friendly, but William still didn't like

40

the idea of Earth being invaded. "In other words you come to steal things," William said.

"Plunder," Hanam said, "plunder's the word. It's traditional."

"Are you going to let me go home?" William asked.

"After we get started plundering, we'll put you down near the place we picked you up," Hanam said. "Meanwhile, just keep out of the way and enjoy your ride. Now I have to get back to work. You may look out the porthole if you like."

William was standing near a round window in the side of the spaceburger. He walked over and looked out. What he saw was amazing. He could see the whole Earth—or most of it. The spaceburger had gotten very high since he had been taken on board. He could see North America, and parts of South America and Europe. It was like the globe in Mr. Wendel's classroom, only the colors were much nicer. Everything was sort of shimmering and glowing, and reflecting the light of the moon. There were clouds like strings of yarn near the earth, and the oceans and big lakes shimmered beautifully. William really liked it. That is, he really liked the Earth—not just the sight he was enjoying. He felt that the Earth was a wonderful

41

place. It was his home and he liked it. It made him feel sort of strange and sad. It made him feel sadder to think that the Earth was going to be invaded, and the people enslaved by these fat spacemen. William wondered what he could do about it—but he was just a kid. There was nothing he could do.

His radio tooth was starting to work again. He had been too busy to pay attention to it, but he had been vaguely aware of the fact that it hadn't been receiving since he came on board the spaceburger. Now, standing near the glass or plastic window, it was starting to pick up faint signals again. William thought that maybe the metal spaceburger stopped the radio waves, but they could pass through the stuff the porthole was made of.

The signals were not as loud and clear as they had been on Earth, but if William clenched his teeth hard, he could make them out. There was the static-language of the spacemen communicating. Moving through space, William wasn't able to make a mental picture of the movements of the spaceships as easily as before. He did get the impression of a lot of activity. There seemed to be more and more of the spaceburgers every minute. William strained to try and see them. Every now and then, he did see a brief flash of reflected light that might have been another spaceburger.

William could also hear the radio station on Earth that had always come through on his tooth. It was very faint, and he had to clench his teeth so hard to hear it that it gave him a headache. He could only keep it up for a few seconds at a time. The radio station was broadcasting news flashes, and they were very interesting.

"Flash—the millions of round objects falling slowly through space are not meteorites as previously thought, but have now been identified as fat men, wearing plaid sport jackets, falling slowly into our atmosphere. Stay tuned to this station for further reports on the amazing story."

The invasion had started. William hoped his mother and father weren't too scared.

"Reports from our affiliated stations seem to indicate that the fat men have started to land. It is estimated that there are hundreds of millions of them still in the sky. The fat men are landing in all parts of the world, but the greatest concentrations appear to be in California and New Jersey."

William looked around. All the fat men, except Hanam,

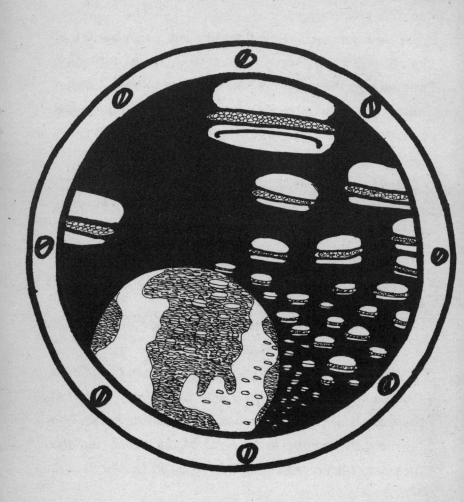

were buttoning their plaid sport jackets, and putting their black plastic-rimmed eyeglasses in their pockets—preparing to jump. Hanam was standing at the controls, operating the spaceburger. A door appeared in the side of the spaceburger, and the crew jumped out. William looked out the porthole and saw the fat men slowly tumbling their way toward Earth.

"There is widespread panic all over Earth, as the hordes of fat men from space continue to land. So far there have been no reports of hostile acts. The governments of all the countries of Earth have asked people to remain calm, and stay in their houses until the invaders express their intentions. We will keep you informed as this amazing story develops."

William could see lots of other spaceburgers now. He saw hundreds of fat spacemen tumble by his porthole. There were spaceburgers dropping spacemen as far as William could see. The only clear places were over the oceans. Everywhere else, there were spacecraft and jumpers. It really was an amazing sight. William couldn't remember ever seeing so many of anything.

"What do these fat men from space want? Is this the beginning of a war? Do they want to conquer the people

of Earth?. . . It appears that, for the moment, they want hamburgers. . . . Crowds of fat men have surrounded roadside hamburger stands throughout the civilized world. . . . They are also consuming great quantities of pizza, and cupcakes wrapped in cellophane . . . and hot dogs . . . and ice cream bars . . . and jelly doughnuts . . . halvah . . . chocolate-covered marshmallows. . . . It seems that the invaders from space are after every sort of junk food. . . . Stand by for further bulletins."

William was starting to get the picture now. He was beginning to understand what sort of pirates these were. The news bulletins were coming faster and faster now.

"No cars, trains, or buses are able to move because of gangs of fat men from space strolling on the roads, eating Twinkies and jumbo cheeseburgers. Airplanes all over the world are grounded by the fat men who are continuing to fall earthward . . ."

"It is next to impossible to make one's way through any of the great cities of Earth because of the clutter of popsicle sticks and empty paper cups in the street . . ."

"Conditions of panic exist in many parts of the United States. Residents of most areas cannot get anything to eat but lean meat, fish, fruit, and vegetables . . ."

*"A late-breaking bulletin from San Anselmo, Califor-
nia—fat men from space broke into a warehouse and ate
sixty thousand frozen tacos . . ."*

*"On State Highway 22 in New Jersey, fat men from
space held two sixteen-year-old girls captive for six hours
at Burger World, until the girls had finished deep-frying
148,000 orders of breaded clams . . ."*

*"The Pentagon announced, a few minutes ago, that
there is no more whipped cream left anywhere on Earth.
General Fred Horsewhistle, speaking for the Joint Chiefs
of Staff, expressed the opinion that it may be necessary to
use nuclear weapons against the fat men, whatever the
cost. Stand by for further bulletins."*

William could see that the situation was very serious.
The fat men from space were eating up all the junk food
on Earth at a fantastic rate. What worried him was what
Hanam had told him about enslaving the people of Earth
to make more junk food for them, after they had eaten
everything on Earth. He was alone in the spaceburger
with Hanam, who was operating the controls, and
munching on a frozen pizza. William wondered if he could
overpower Hanam in some way, and get to Earth to warn
everybody about what was going to happen next. He

47

decided there was no way. He didn't know how to operate the spaceburger, and besides Hanam was much bigger than he was. William just looked out of the porthole, and listened to his tooth.

"In Cleveland, Ohio, spacemen are preparing to dynamite the locked doors of the White Palace frozen hamburger vault, containing one-fourth of the hamburgers on Earth. Mankind will never recover from this massive onslaught against its hamburger reserves."

The hours passed, and the news flashes continued. William had taken a nap, and Hanam had let him make himself a milkshake and a frozen Mexican dinner. When William looked out the porthole, the fat men were still continuing to fall through the sky.

"In Coney Island, New York, hot dog men made a brave attempt to defend Nathan's famous hot dog stand against a large gang of fat spacemen. After a fierce battle, lasting several hours, the hot dog men were overpowered, and tied up with strings of their own hot dogs, forced to watch while the fat men devoured all the steamed corn, and French-fried potatoes. This is one of the most heartbreaking and tragic stories of the current emergency, and citizens of Brooklyn have already stated their inten-

tion to erect a monument to the brave hot dog men when normal conditions return . . ."

"A news flash—the White House has been invaded by the spacemen who have carried off the President's private store of frozen Milky Way bars. As soon as Congress can make its way through the welter of empty fish-and-chips boxes that are obstructing traffic in the Capitol, it is expected that war will be declared against wherever the fat men come from."

William thought this was getting serious. "You spacemen had better leave, before war is declared," he said to Hanam.

"That doesn't worry us," Hanam said. "You don't have any weapons that we can't eat."

It looked extremely bad for Earth. William had just heard that the fat men had found the Holloway's Milk Duds factory in Chicago, and cleaned it out. Giant chocolate factories in Hershey, Pennsylvania, were deserted. Not a crumb or a person was left. Whole populations were making their way out of cities, stumbling on foot through the piles of wastepaper, cartons, and wrappers. Families tried to escape into the hills or the country, carrying a bag of marshmallows, or a Three Musketeers bar. In almost every case, squads of fat men intercepted the fugitives, and took away their last bit of junk food.

William knew that when the spacemen had gobbled all the cheeseburgers and pizzas and doughnuts, they would enslave the people of Earth and make them produce more things for the invaders to eat. It looked hopeless. It looked dismal. He looked at Hanam. Hanam was licking his fingers. He had just finished an ice-cream pop and a bottle of birch beer. He was idly working the levers and buttons that controlled the spaceburger. An orange light was flashing on the instrument panel, and a high-pitched beeper was beeping. It seemed to be a signal of some sort. Hanam shot a nervous look at William, and went back to minding the controls.

William looked out the porthole. There was a tremendous stirring in the space above Earth. It looked to William as though the fat men were falling upward. They were falling upward! They were tumbling up from Earth, just the way they had tumbled down. William looked at Hanam. Hanam looked worried and preoccupied. "What's happening?" William asked. Hanam didn't answer.

William tried to tune in on the static-language. There

was so much talking going on that William had a hard time making out what was being said. Something about a potato pancake—the usual topic. Why all this activity, and excitement? William clenched and tuned in the radio station. *"More reports are coming in every minute to the effect that the spacemen appear to be leaving Earth. This radio station will keep you informed of this surprising development."*

There was a thumping on the outside of the space-burger. A door appeared and first one, then another of the crew tumbled in. They seemed excited. Another thumping, and more spacemen came aboard. "What's going on?" William asked.

"We're leaving," Hanam said. "As soon as the rest of the crew come aboard, we'll be off for another solar system. You see, a message just came through from Sargon. There is a report of a giant potato pancake launched in space in the vicinity of the planet Ziegler. We're going to go after it. It sounds like the biggest potato pancake ever sighted."

"What about me?" William asked. "You said you were going to take me home."

"There won't be time for that," Hanam said. "A potato

pancake like this, a wild one floating in space, turns up once in fifty years. You'll have to come along."

"But when will you take me home?" William asked.

"We might come this way in six or seven hundred years," Hanam answered. "We'll drop you off then."

"Six or seven hundred years!" William said. "I'll be an old man by then! I want to go home now!"

"I don't see how we can do that," Hanam said. "We have to leave as soon as the last two crew members come aboard."

"You promised to take me home!" William shouted. "I don't want to go with you. I don't want to go chasing a wild potato pancake in outer space for seven hundred years! I want to go home right now!"

"Well, the only thing I can suggest is that you float down," Hanam said.

"I don't know how to float down," William said.

"There's nothing to it, if you have a spacejacket," Hanam said. "We can give you a spare, and drop you right away."

Hanam reached into a locker and pulled out a plaid sport jacket. "Here, try this on," he said.

William tried the jacket on. It was about fifty sizes too

large. It came right down to his feet.

"All you have to do is jump," Hanam said. A door appeared.

"I'm not sure I understand," William said. Hanam pushed him out the door.

Once he got used to it, William liked falling through space. The only thing that bothered him was that he couldn't tell if he was falling fast or slow. As he tumbled down, droves of fat spacemen passed him, falling in the other direction—falling upward. It took William quite a while to fall through space, and while he was falling he thought things over. If he understood it correctly, the plaid sport jacket was supposed to break his fall in some way. He hoped that was the way it worked. Otherwise, he was going to make a little hole in the ground when he hit.

William looked at the map of North America below him. He wondered if he would land anywhere near home. Gradually the map turned into a model railroad landscape of mountains and trees, towns and lakes. He knew he was falling slowly, like a snowflake, now. He felt like a snowflake—it was cold, high up in the atmosphere. William passed through clouds, slowly. The clouds were wet and unpleasant, not at all the way William thought they would

feel. He pulled the plaid spacejacket tight around him.

As William got closer to Earth, he could see individual houses and cars. Now and then a few spacemen would float up past him. William guessed that most of them had already returned to their spaceburgers. William realized that his float-down was almost over, and he felt a little sad. It had been the best part of the whole experience.

William floated down, and landed on the sidewalk in front of his house! He gave a little push with his feet, and floated over the house into the backyard. He did one more experimental jump, straight up, of about a hundred feet, landed lightly, took off the spacejacket, folded it neatly, and went into the house.

Everything was normal inside the house, except that the door had been ripped off the freezer. William's mother told him later that some fat men had broken in and taken all the TV dinners, the sugar-coated breakfast cereal, and the instant breakfast powder.

William's parents were glad to see him. They had been worried about him, of course, but during the emergency it had been impossible to get in touch with the police. William's father had tried to go out and look for him, but he never got past the enormous piles of Big Mac boxes in the road. So William's mother and father just sat at home during most of the invasion from outer space, eating the shredded wheat and lettuce that the spacemen had left them, and hoping their son was all right.

William put the spacejacket carefully away in his closet. He didn't have much time to enjoy it. School and most kinds of work had been suspended for several weeks, and the people on Earth devoted themselves to a massive effort to clean-up the litter. William and his parents were out every day with rakes and shovels, and came home tired every night to their green salad and whole-grain bread, milk, and sometimes meat. William and his parents got to enjoy the clean-up work, and even the experience of living without cheeseburgers and pizza. After the clean-up was finished, the government announced it would be at least a year before soda pop, taco chips, and a lot of other things were once again in general supply. There was almost no sugar anywhere on Earth, which turned out to be much less of a hardship than people expected.

William's parents seemed to have forgotten about the radio tooth. William didn't see any point in mentioning it to them. It still worked, although not as well as it had before the shock from the metal fence, and the adventure in the spaceburger. Sometimes the tooth would be silent for days at a time, and sometimes it would play fairly well. When William went to the dentist a year later, the tooth hadn't played for almost a month, and Dr. Horwitz thought it would probably stop playing altogether after a while. He also told William that he had no new cavities—a common occurrence worldwide, since sugar was still scarce.

But the radio tooth was not entirely dead. Some nights it would play quite well, and on special nights—ones that were clear and cold—William could hear, behind the Barry Garble show, a kind of rhythmic static that was almost like a language.